4-19

A Beginning-to-Read Book

Dear Dragon Helps Out

by Margaret Hillert

Illustrated by David Schimmell

NorwoodHouse Press

DEAR CAREGIVER, The *Beginning-to-Read* series is a carefully written collection of classic readers you may remember from your own childhood. Each book features text comprised of common sight words to provide your child ample practice reading the words that appear most frequently in written text. The many additional details in the pictures enhance the story and offer the opportunity for you to help your child expand oral language and develop comprehension.

Begin by reading the story to your child, followed by letting him or her read familiar words and soon your child will be able to read the story independently. At each step of the way, be sure to praise your reader's efforts to build his or her confidence as an independent reader. Discuss the pictures and encourage your child to make connections between the story and his or her own life. At the end of the story, you will find reading activities and a word list that will help your child practice and strengthen beginning reading skills.

Above all, the most important part of the reading experience is to have fun and enjoy it!

Shannon Cannon

Shannon Cannon,
Literacy Consultant

Norwood House Press • P.O. Box 316598 • Chicago, Illinois 60631
For more information about Norwood House Press please visit our website at *www.norwoodhousepress.com* or call 866-565-2900.

LIBRARY OF CONGRESS CATALOGING-IN-PUBLICATION DATA
Hillert, Margaret.
Dear dragon helps out / by Margaret Hillert ; illustrated by David Schimmell.
p. cm. -- (A beginning-to-read book)
Summary: "A boy and his pet dragon find the joy in being helpful to others"--Provided by publisher.
ISBN-13: 978-1-59953-505-0 (library edition : alk. paper)
ISBN-10: 1-59953-505-X (library edition : alk. paper)
ISBN-13: 978-1-60357-385-6 (e-book)
ISBN-10: 1-60357-385-2 (e-book)
[1. Helpfulness--Fiction. 2. Dragons--Fiction.] I. Schimmell, David, ill.
II. Title. PZ7.H558Iq 2012
[E]--dc23
2011038948
Manufactured in the United States of America in North Mankato, Minnesota
280R–052015

Mother, Mother.
I did a lot of things.
I was a big help.
Now I can help you.

I will go with you.

That was fun.
But I want to go [illegible] eat something.

Oh dear dragon, here I am with you.
Here you are with me.
It is so good to have friends.

READING REINFORCEMENT

The following activities support the findings of the National Reading Panel that determined the most effective components for reading instruction are: Phonemic Awareness, Phonics, Vocabulary, Fluency, and Text Comprehension.

Phonemic Awareness: The /h/ sound

Deletion: Ask your child to say the following words without the beginning /**h**/ sound:

hat - /h/ = at
hit - /h/ = it
hand - /h/ = and
hop - /h/ = op
his - /h/ = is
hair - /h/ = air
ham - /h/ = am
harm - /h/ = arm

Phonics: The letter Hh

1. Demonstrate how to form the letters **H** and **h** for your child.
2. Have your child practice writing **H** and **h** at least three times each.
3. Ask your child to point to the words in the book that start with the letter **h**.
4. Write down the following words and ask your child to circle the letter **h** in each word:

happy
help
hair
hut
hand
father
the
house
mother
home
there
where
hug
how
here
have

Vocabulary: Baby Animal Names

1. Explain to your child that baby animals often have different names than their parents.
2. Write each of the following words on separate index cards:

rabbit/bunny	squirrel/pup	skunk/kit	tiger/cub
frog/tadpole	cow/calf	pig/piglet	dog/puppy
cat/kitten	duck/duckling	chicken/chick	goat/kid
goose/gosling	kangaroo/joey	deer/fawn	horse/foal

3. Place the adult and baby names next to each other and read the words to your child.
4. Mix up the words.
5. Work with your child to match the adult/baby animal pairs.

Fluency: Choral Reading

1. Reread the story to your child at least two more times while your child tracks the print by running a finger under the words as they are read. Ask your child to read the words he or she knows with you.
2. Reread the story aloud together. Be careful to read at a rate that your child can keep up with.
3. Repeat choral reading and allow your child to be the lead reader and ask him or her to change from a whisper to a loud voice while you follow along and change your voice.

Text Comprehension: Discussion Time

1. Ask your child to retell the sequence of events in the story.
2. To check comprehension, ask your child the following questions:
   - What are some of the things that the boy did to help other people?
   - Why do you think the cat did not need help with the baby cat?
   - What do the boy and his friend do when they are finished working?
   - What are some things that you do to help other people?

WORD LIST

Dear Dragon Helps Out uses the 90 words listed below.

This list can be used to practice reading the words that appear in the text. You may wish to write the words on index cards and use them to help your child build automatic word recognition. Regular practice with these words will enhance your child's fluency in reading connected text.

a
am
and
are
at

baby
bag
be
big
boy
brown
but

can
cat
come

dear
did
do
dog

down
dragon

eat

Father
for
friend(s)
fun

get
go
good
guess

have
he
help
here
home
how

I
in
is
it
it's

jump

leaves
likes
little
long
look
lot

make
me
Mother
my

not
nothing

now
of
oh
on
out
over

play
preety

red

see
she
so
something

take
team
that
the
then

there
these
things
this
to
too

walk
want(s)
was
we
what
where
will
with
work

yellow
yes
you

ABOUT THE AUTHOR

Margaret Hillert has written over 80 books for children who are just learning to read. Her books have been translated into many different languages and over a million children throughout the world have read her books. She first started writing poetry as a child and has continued to write for children and adults throughout her life. A first grade teacher for 34 years, Margaret is now retired from teaching and lives in Michigan where she likes to write, take walks in the morning, and care for her three cats.

Photograph by Glenna Washburn

ABOUT THE ADVISER

Shannon Cannon contributed the activities pages that appear in this book. Shannon serves as a literacy consultant and provides staff development to help improve reading instruction. She is a frequent presenter at educational conferences and workshops. Prior to this she worked as an elementary school teacher and as president of a curriculum publishing company.

PDO

You are pretty good too.
We make a good team!

Boy!
You are good at this.

Yes, yes.
That will be fun.

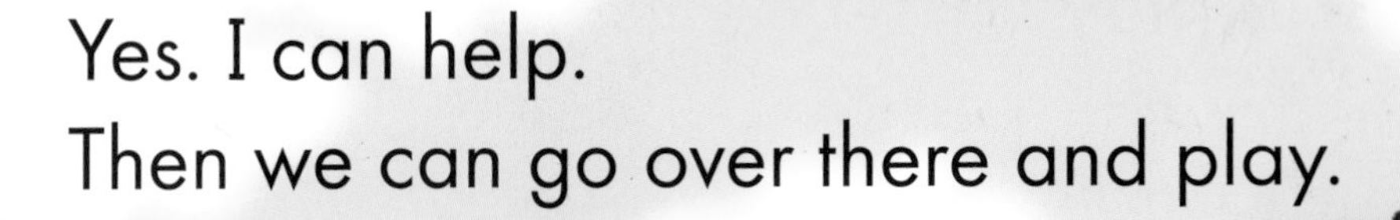
Yes. I can help.
Then we can go over there and play.

It is fun to play here.
but we have to work.

Oh, I did not see you.
Do you want to help too?

What pretty leaves.
Red and yellow leaves.

Now I can do work for you, Father
I can get these leaves in the bag.

Come on now, dog.
I will take you home.

Oh, there she is.
Down, dog, down.
Do not jump.
We do not have to help.
The mother will help the baby.

There is a little brown baby cat.
Where is the mother?

Yes. Come on, dog.
We will take a good, long walk.

Can you take my dog for
a walk? He likes to walk.

Here I am.
How can I help you?

Oh, look out here.
It's a friend.
I guess she wants you.

That is not good.
It is good to have
something to do.

Mother, Mother.
I have nothing to do.
What can I do?